MALIKA'S CROWN

WRITTEN BY
Shani Major

ILLUSTRATED BY
Kathrine Gutkovskiy

smajorbooks.com

Cover Illustration by Kathrine Gutkovskiy

Author Photo | Chris Smith – SmithShot Photography

ISBN: 979-8-218-00006-6
Printed in United States

For my daughters,
Amira and Imani

The doorbell rang. Malika flew down the stairs and ran smack into her mother.

"Slow down, Malika," she said with a smile.

"Sorry, Mommy."

Malika grinned as she peaked around her mother's legs to greet her first guest.

"Alexis!"

Cali and Taylor were holding hands as they bounced toward the door—not far behind Alexis. Their mothers greeted one another with hugs as the girls waited patiently to be excused.

"You can go, girls," Malika's mom said. "But try not to be too loud—Malika's grandmother is taking a nap." Malika and her friends ran up the stairs in a flurry of tulle.

It was teatime! Well, not real tea. It was a pretend tea party that they had been planning for days. Malika's play table was decorated with fancy dishes and silverware fit for a queen. One of her stuffed animals sat in each chair—saving the seats for each of the girls.

Malika gently moved each stuffed animal and guided her friends to their seats. As they sipped their tea and dined on their make-believe snacks, the sunlight bounced off Malika's crown creating tiny rainbows across the table.

Cali asked Malika, "May I hold your crown?"

Taylor said, "I want to wear it!"

"Me, too!" exclaimed Alexis.

Malika stomped her foot and said,
"But I'm not done with it!"

The other girls said in unison,
"Why can't we see it?"

"I should have brought my own
crown!" Alexis huffed.

"Little ladies, what's all the commotion?" The girls turned quickly to see Malika's grandmother standing in the doorway. Malika's eyes widened, "I'm sorry Gammy, we didn't mean to wake you up."

"Not to worry, my dear," she said as she made her way across the room and sat in the rocking chair, placing her cane across her lap.

"Out with it. What's the matter?"

The girls all spoke at once. "We want to see Malika's crown. She isn't sharing Gammy."

Gammy raised her eyebrows in Malika's direction. Malika was pouting.

"Come, girls," Gammy waved them over.

The girls shuffled toward Gammy and made themselves comfortable at her feet. "Now you know... "

Gammy gently removed Malika's crown and examined it before finishing.

"This crown is lovely, but each of you have your own. The ones you have are far more beautiful."

The girls looked at each other confused. "Gammy, what do you mean?" Malika asked.

"Your tresses, your locs, your hair. Long ago in Africa, your ancestors wore their hair in beautiful designs. Their crowns were a symbol of royalty."

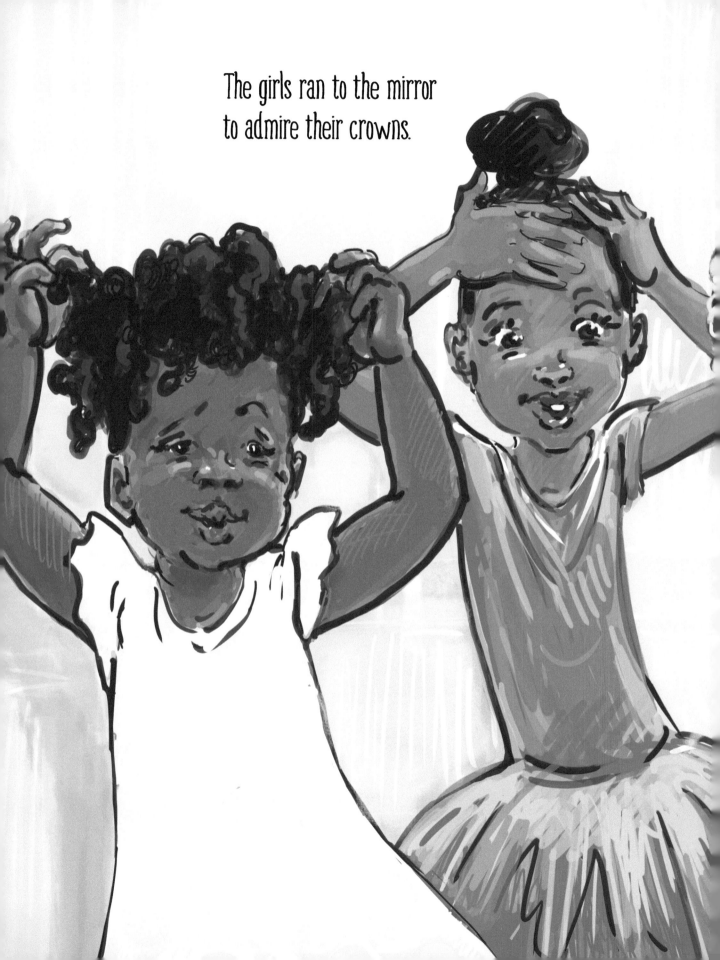

The girls ran to the mirror
to admire their crowns.

Gammy crept out of the room. "Have fun, girls." she called from the hall. Gammy smiled as she kept Malika's crown for herself. After all, she was the true queen of the house.

Shani Major

Shani Major is a third-grade teacher, mother of three, and author from Atlanta, Georgia. She writes children's books based on her experiences as a mother and teacher. Shani is a passionate reader with a mission to share the importance of literacy. She loves to read stories aloud with her children and students and introduce them to her favorites.

You can find out more about Shani Major and her work at smajorbooks.com.

Kathrine Gutkovskiy

Kathrine, mom of two wonderful boys, is an illustrator living in Los Alamos, New Mexico. She received her art education at The Art Students League of New York. When she isn't illustrating, she enjoys spending time with her family and teaching her kids drawing. She believes that visiting art museums is a great way to relax and find inspiration for new projects.